SHAKESPEARE'S THE MERCHANT OF VENICE

AN AQA ESSAY WRITING GUIDE

R. P. DAVIS

Copyright © 2020 Accolade Tuition Ltd
Published by Accolade Tuition Ltd
71-75 Shelton Street
Covent Garden
London WC2H 9JQ
www.accoladetuition.com
info@accoladetuition.com

ISBN 978-1-9163735-5-6

FIRST EDITION
1 3 5 7 9 10 8 6 4 2

For Robert.

CONTENTS

FOREWORD

In your GCSE English Literature exam, you will be presented with an extract from Shakespeare's *The Merchant of Venice* and a question that asks you to offer both a close analysis of the extract plus a commentary of the play as a whole. Of course, there are many methods one *might* use to tackle this style of question. However, there is one particular technique which, due to its sophistication, most readily allows students to unlock the highest marks: namely, **the thematic method**.

To be clear, this study guide is *not* intended to walk you through the play scene-by-scene: there are many great guides out there that do just that. No, this guide, by sifting through a series of mock exam questions, will demonstrate *how* to organise a response thematically and thus write a stellar essay: a skill we believe no other study guide adequately covers!

I have encountered students who have structured their essays all sorts of ways: some by writing about the extract line by line, others by identifying various language techniques and giving each its own paragraph. The method I'm advocating, on the other hand, involves picking out three to four themes that will allow you to holistically answer the question: these three to four themes will become the three to four content paragraphs of your essay, cushioned between a brief introduction and conclusion. Ideally, these themes will follow from one to the next to create a flowing argument. Within each of these thematic paragraphs, you can then ensure you are jumping through the mark scheme's hoops.

So to break things down further, each thematic paragraph will include various point-scoring components. In each paragraph, you will quote from the extract, offer analyses of these quotes, then discuss how the specific language techniques you have identified illustrate the theme you're discussing. In each paragraph, you will also discuss how other parts of the play further illustrate the theme (or even complicate it). And in each, you will comment on the era in which the play was written and how that helps to understand the chosen theme.

Don't worry if this all feels daunting. Throughout this guide, I will be illustrating in great detail – by means of examples – how to build an essay of this kind.

The Shakespearian equivalent of a selfie.

The beauty of the thematic approach is that, once you have your themes, you suddenly have a direction and a trajectory, and this makes essay writing a whole lot easier. However, it must also be noted that extracting themes in the first place is something students often find tricky. I have come across many candidates who understand the extract and the play inside out; but when they are presented with a question under exam conditions, and the pressure kicks in, they find it tough to break their response down into themes. The fact of the matter is: the process is a *creative* one and the best themes require a bit of imagination.

In this guide, I shall take seven different exam-style questions, coupled with extracts from the play, and put together a plan for each – a plan that illustrates in detail how we will be satisfying the mark scheme's criteria. Please do keep in mind that, when operating under timed conditions, your plans will necessarily be less detailed than those that appear in this volume.

Now, you might be asking whether three or four themes is best. The truth is, you should do whatever you feel most comfortable with: the examiner is looking for an original, creative answer, and not sitting there counting the themes. So if you think you are quick enough to cover four, then great. However, if you would rather do three to make sure you do each theme justice, that's also fine. I sometimes suggest that my student pick four themes, but make the fourth one smaller – sort of like an afterthought, or an observation that turns things on their head. That way, if they feel they won't have time to explore this fourth theme in its own right, they can always give it a quick mention in the conclusion instead.

The Globe Theatre in London. It was built on the site of the original, which was burnt down in 1613.

Before I move forward in earnest, I believe it to be worthwhile to run through the four Assessment Objectives the exam board want you to cover in your response – if only to demonstrate how effective the thematic response can be. I would argue that the first Assessment Objective (AO1) – the one that wants candidates to 'read, understand and respond to texts' and which is worth 12 of the total 34 marks up for grabs – will be wholly satisfied by selecting strong themes, then fleshing them out with quotes. Indeed, when it comes to identifying the top-scoring candidates for AO1, the mark scheme explicitly tells examiners to look for a 'critical, exploratory, conceptualised response' that makes 'judicious use of precise references' – the word 'concept' is a synonym of theme, and 'judicious references' simply refers to quotes that appropriately support the theme you've chosen.

The second Assessment Objective (AO2) – which is also responsible for 12 marks – asks students to 'analyse the language, form and structure used by a writer to create meanings and effects, using relevant subject terminology where appropriate.' As noted, you will already be quoting from the play as you back up your themes, and it is a natural progression to then analyse the language techniques used. In fact, this is far more effective than simply observing language techniques (personification here, alliteration there), because by discussing how the language techniques relate to and shape the theme, you will also be demonstrating how the writer 'create[s] meanings and effects.'

Now, in my experience, language analysis is the most important element of AO2 – perhaps 8 of the 12 marks will go towards language analysis. You will also notice, however, that AO2 asks students to comment on 'form and structure.' Again, the thematic approach has your back – because though simply jamming in a point on form or structure will feel jarring, when you bring these points up while discussing a theme, as a means to further a thematic argument, you will again organically be discussing the way it 'create[s] meanings and effects.'

AO3 requires you to 'show understanding of the relationships between texts and the contexts in which they were written' and is responsible for a more modest 6 marks in total. These are easy enough to weave into a thematic argument; indeed, the theme gives the student a chance to bring up context in a relevant and fitting way. After all, you don't want it to look like you've just shoehorned a contextual factoid into the mix.

Finally, you have AO4 – known also as "spelling and grammar." There are four marks up for grabs here. Truth be told, this guide is not geared towards AO4. My advice? Make sure you are reading plenty of books and articles, because the more you read, the better your spelling and grammar will be. Also, before the exam, perhaps make a list of words you struggle to spell but often find yourself using in essays, and commit them to memory.

| The Globe Theatre's interior.

My hope is that this book, by demonstrating how to tease out themes from an extract, will help you feel more confident in doing so yourself. I believe it is also worth mentioning that the themes I have picked out are by no means definitive. Asked the very same question, someone else may pick out different themes, and write an answer that is just as good (if not better!). Obviously the exam is not likely to be fun – my memory of them is pretty much the exact opposite. But still, this is one of the very few chances that you will get at GCSE level to actually be creative. And to my mind at least, that was always more enjoyable – if *enjoyable* is the right word – than simply demonstrating that I had memorised loads of facts.

READ THE FOLLOWING EXTRACT FROM
ACT 1 SCENE 1 OF THE MERCHANT OF
VENICE AND ANSWER THE QUESTION
THAT FOLLOWS.

At this point in the play, Bassanio is trying to convince Antonio to bankroll his voyage to Belmont in order to court Portia.

BASSANIO
In Belmont is a lady richly left;
And she is fair, and, fairer than that word,
Of wondrous virtues: sometimes from her eyes
I did receive fair speechless messages:
Her name is Portia, nothing undervalued
To Cato's daughter, Brutus' Portia:
Nor is the wide world ignorant of her worth,
For the four winds blow in from every coast
Renowned suitors, and her sunny locks
Hang on her temples like a golden fleece;
Which makes her seat of Belmont Colchos' strand,
And many Jasons come in quest of her.
O my Antonio, had I but the means
To hold a rival place with one of them,
I have a mind presages me such thrift,

That I should questionless be fortunate!

Starting with this speech, explain how far you think Shakespeare presents Bassanio as being in love with Portia.

Write about:

• **how Shakespeare presents Bassanio in this extract**

• **how Shakespeare presents Bassanio in the play as a whole**

Introduction

It's important to keep the introduction short and sweet, but also to ensure it packs a punch – after all, you only have one chance to make a first impression on the examiner. I recommend starting the introduction with a short comment on historical context to score early AO3 marks. I would then suggest that you very quickly summarize the thematic gist of your essay.

'Given the Elizabethan era's profound interest in medieval culture, it is unsurprising that medieval courtly love ideals figure prominently in Shakespeare's works. In this extract, Bassanio seeks to communicate his love for Portia not only by describing her in transcendental terms, but also by framing his courtship as a daring quest that implicitly casts him as an archetypal courtly lover. Yet these overtures of affection are powerfully undercut by Bassanio's materialistic motives and lack of lovesickness.'

Theme/Paragraph One: Perhaps most striking in this extract is Bassanio's blatant profiteering, which threatens to reduce his pursuit of Portia to a mere transaction.

- Shakespeare makes the structural choice of having Bassanio invoke Portia's wealth before all else: she is, Bassanio informs Antonio, 'a lady richly left.' That she has been 'left' almost seems to imply that Antonio sees her as if an inanimate object ready to be retrieved, while the half-rhyme between 'lady' and 'richly' further accentuates how Antonio sees her wealth as integral to her identity. Antonio continues in these blunt terms, stacking up Portia's wealth to that of her Roman namesake, 'Brutus's Portia.' The classical allusion in this context implies that it is her wealth first and foremost that Antonio considers as being of epic proportions.[1] Moreover, Shakespeare ends the first line of this comparison – 'Her name is Portia, nothing undervalued' – with an unstressed hyperbeat that overruns the iambic pentameter, the excess syllable mirroring Portia's excessive wealth.[2] [*AO1 for advancing the argument with a judiciously selected quote; AO2 for the close analysis of the language and for discussing how structure shapes meaning*].
- With a second classical allusion, Bassanio goes a step further, equating Portia with the 'golden fleece' that Jason sought in Greek myth: a comparison that yet

again frames her as an object one seeks for self-enrichment.

- *Elsewhere in the play*: Crucially, Antonio does not seek to conceal his profiteering: he freely concedes that his 'chief care / Is to come fairly off from the great debts' he has amassed. Indeed, Portia seems to intuit the transactional nature of their relationship, observing in Act 3 Scene 2, that Antonio was 'dear bought.' [*AO1 for advancing the argument with a judiciously selected quote*].

Theme/Paragraph Two: While Bassanio's blunt financial motives suggest insincerity, they are counterbalanced by a transcendent portrayal of Portia – a portrayal that borrows from the language of courtly love and arguably suggests genuine ardour.

- As Bassanio parses Portia's looks, he finds words inadequate to express her beauty – a common motif in courtly romance. Bassanio observes that Portia's appearance is at once 'fair,' and yet also 'fairer than that word' can convey. If, as Antony proclaims in Shakespeare's *Antony and Cleopatra*, 'there's beggary in the love that can be reckoned,' it seems here that it is Portia's fairness that is beyond reckoning – it is beyond the reach of description. Significantly, fair skin was considered synonymous with beauty in Elizabethan England (a racial bias further indicated by Portia's scathing assessment of the dark-skinned Morocco). [*AO1 for advancing the argument with a judiciously selected quote; AO3 for placing the text in relevant historical and literary context].*

- However, the words 'fair' and 'fairer' refer also to Portia's capacity for virtue, as confirmed by Bassanio's assertion that Portia is 'of wondrous virtues.' Yet if Portia's fairness is beyond Bassanio's ability to describe, it seems that when she exhibits those traits, she does so in a way that also transcends speech: Bassanio observes that 'from her eyes / I did receive fair speechless messages.' Language is inadequate not only for describing her fairness, but also as a vessel for her 'fair...messages,' which she can better transmit 'from her eyes.' [*AO1 for advancing the argument with a judiciously selected quote; AO2 for the close analysis of the language*].

- *Elsewhere in the play*: Yet although it might be argued that Bassanio's language connotes sincerity, it should be noted that Morocco – who Shakespeare dispatches in short order, as if to imply his feelings lacked the potency to stay the course – expresses his sentiments for Portia in similar terms: he calls her 'fair Portia;' a 'mortal-breathing saint.' While this may not utterly subvert Bassanio's words, it opens the possibility that Bassanio is just another chancer aping the language of courtly love.

Theme/Paragraph Three: By framing the proposed courtship as an epic quest, Bassanio casts himself as a suitor in the courtly love tradition, thus implicitly telegraphing the seriousness of his feelings for Portia.

- Although the allusion to Jason's quest points to Bassanio's materialism, it also serves to cast Bassanio's courtship, and the voyage it entails, as a heroic 'quest,' characterised by difficulties akin to those faced by Jason. In the courtly tradition, the knight undergoes quests of trials and tribulations to prove his love for his beloved. By conveying the quest-like nature of his courtship, Bassanio thus seeks to establish the sincerity of his love for Portia. That Bassanio invokes other suitors, and talks of holding a 'rival place,' adds an element of competition that further reinforces the air of courtly quest. [*AO1 for advancing the argument with a judiciously selected quote*].
- <u>*Elsewhere in the play*</u>: However, Bassanio's depiction of this voyage is powerfully undercut when Portia later instructs Balthazar to travel on 'the common ferry / Which trades to Venice.' The audience abruptly realises that Bassanio's journey is *not* a daring undertaking against 'four winds,' but a prosaic commute that can be conducted on a 'common ferry' – a revelation that subverts the voyage as a stamp of authenticity for Bassanio's love. [*AO1 for advancing the argument with a judiciously selected quote; AO2 for the close analysis of the language*].

Theme/Paragraph Four: In the courtly tradition, another marker of sincerity is lovesickness: the lover suffers when apart from his beloved. However, Bassanio exhibits no such lovesickness for Portia.

- When exiled from Verona, Shakespeare's Romeo

describes the prospect of being separated from Juliet as 'torture, hell itself.' In contrast, however, Bassanio fails to exhibit the discomfort one would expect from a courtly lover separated from his would-be belle. The closest Bassanio comes to suffering over Portia is when he is faced with the casket challenge in Belmont. Yet although he describes himself as 'on the rack' – a reference to an Elizabethan torture device – there is little to indicate that the suffering is to do with the prospect of losing access to Portia as opposed to her wealth.[3] [*AO1 for advancing the argument with a judiciously selected quote; AO3 for invoking relevant historical and literary context*].

- Curiously, however, the audience *does* in this extract get a hint of the sort of language usually associated with courtly lovesickness when Bassanio exclaims: 'O my Antonio.' One might note that a sense of lovesickness pervades Antonio and Bassanio's relationship. The play opens with Antonio suffering with symptoms resembling lovesickness; Antonio sends Bassanio off with 'his eye...big with tears;' and Bassanio is so distressed by Shylock's entrapment of Antonio that he claims he would sacrifice 'life itself, my wife, and all the world' to free Antonio. This mutual lovesickness, bordering on homoeroticism, highlights the relative inadequacy of Bassanio's love for Portia, suggesting the play's true love story is between Antonio and Bassanio. [*AO1 for advancing the argument with a judiciously selected quote; AO2 for the close analysis of the language*].

Conclusion

I feel confident that our essay has enough in the way of thematic discussion to be satisfying the exam board's AO1 stipulations; so, instead of bringing in any fresh themes, I shall invoke some literary context to ensure that the examiner has no excuse to dock me any marks on the AO3 front, and then shall sum up the essay's thematic discussion:

'In Chaucer's *The Franklin's Tale* – a text Shakespeare knew well, and which also features sinister bargains and risky sea-voyaging – the young Aurelius professes lovesickness for Dorigen, yet sleeps with an ease that suggests it may be an act. Similarly, while Bassanio describes Portia in transcendental terms, Shakespeare, by putting near identical language in Morocco's mouth, subtly implies that Bassanio's love for Portia may be shallow and unexceptional. Yet whereas the audience is left uncertain of Bassanio's feelings for Portia, his love for Antonio – evidenced by the frank lovesickness and the surrender of his engagement ring on Antonio's behalf – is stamped indelibly on the mind.'

A statue of Shakespeare in Stratford-upon-Avon, the town in which he was born.

ESSAY PLAN TWO

READ THE FOLLOWING EXTRACT FROM
ACT 1 SCENE 3 OF THE MERCHANT OF
VENICE AND ANSWER THE QUESTION
THAT FOLLOWS.

At this point in the play, Bassanio is trying to borrow money from Shylock by using Antonio's assets as collateral.

SHYLOCK

Antonio is a good man.

BASSANIO

Have you heard any imputation to the contrary?

SHYLOCK

Oh, no, no, no, no: my meaning in saying he is a good
 man is to have you understand me that he is
 sufficient. Yet his means are in supposition: he hath
 an argosy bound to Tripolis, another to the Indies; I
 understand moreover, upon the Rialto, he hath a
 third at Mexico, a fourth for England, and other
 ventures he hath, squandered abroad. But ships are
 but boards, sailors but men: there be land-rats and
 water-rats, water-thieves and land-thieves, I mean
 pirates, and then there is the peril of waters, winds

and rocks. The man is, notwithstanding, sufficient. Three thousand ducats; I think I may take his bond.

Starting with this passage, explain how far you think Shakespeare presents Shylock as a rational character.

Write about:

• **how far Shakespeare presents Shylock as rational in this extract**

• **how far Shakespeare presents Shylock as rational in the play as a whole**

Introduction

As I have suggested before, we want to start with an early AO3 point; then we want to follow up with a quick nod to the themes you have in mind:

"Throughout Shakespeare's works, mankind's capacity for reason is touted as the quality that sets the species apart: 'What a piece of work is a man! how noble in reason!' Hamlet proclaims. Although many characters in *The Merchant of Venice* seek to portray Shylock as subhuman, he is in many respects – in his understanding of the logic of money and law, for instance – a highly rational actor. However, while there is surely a rationale behind his vengeful actions, the sheer zeal with which Shylock pursues his revenge arguably represents a unique form of irrationality."

Theme/Paragraph One: Shylock might be described as rational insofar as he is portrayed in this extract as viewing the world through the prism of money, and thus the cold, hard logic it represents.

- The miscommunication that kicks off this extract captures a clash of worldviews: Shylock's remark that Antonio is a 'good man' is construed by Bassanio as implicitly calling into question Antonio's moral rectitude (he bristles in response: 'Have you heard any imputation to the contrary?'). However, Shylock explains that his use of 'good' refers *not* to morality, but economics: it is a question of whether somebody is 'sufficient' to honour a financial commitment. If money is a mechanism that seeks to quantify and measure, to apportion everything its proper value, then viewing the world through its prism might be considered the height of rationality. [*AO1 for advancing the argument with a judiciously selected quote*].

- That the quibble centres on the word 'good' is particularly telling: Shylock's worldview here is not based in *good* and bad, but *goods* and services. Given that Elizabethan society frequently stereotyped Jews as avaricious and money obsessed, it is perhaps little surprise that Shakespeare portrays Shylock in this way. [*AO2 for the close analysis of*

*the language; AO3 for invoking relevant historical
context*].

- *Elsewhere in the play*: Shylock seems just as focused
  on economic concerns at other points in the play, too:
  when Jessica abandons Shylock, for example, his
  concern is more to do with the money she stole than
  the fact she left. That said, it would be disingenuous
  to claim that Shylock views the world *only* through
  this lens: his plaintive comment on learning that
  Jessica had given away his engagement ring – 'it was
  my turquoise; I had it of Leah when I was a bachelor'
  – indicates that the sentimental value was at the
  forefront of his mind. [*AO1 for advancing the
  argument with a judiciously selected quote*].

**Theme/Paragraph Two: Although Shylock's finan-
cial-mindedness might indicate rationality, there
is a sense in this speech – and in others that
Shylock delivers – that the internal logic he
deploys is unsound.**

- The main bulk of Shylock's speech in this extract is an
  enumeration of the risks Antonio represents as a
  guarantor for Bassanio's loan. He observes that, since
  Antonio's wealth is not in Venice but dispersed out at
  sea ('bound to Tripolis, another to the Indies...'), it has
  become merely hypothetical: a 'supposition.' He then
  enumerates exactly why this circumstance is so risky,
  citing dangers both human ('water-thieves and land-
  thieves') and natural. Indeed, the form – long
  sentences, comprising of multiple clauses – enhances
  the sense of a building argument. However, despite

spelling all of this out in meticulous detail – even using the word 'squandered' to suggest that Antonio's wealth is as good as lost – his logic suddenly seems to short-circuit, and he pronounces that Antonio 'is, notwithstanding, sufficient.' [*AO1 for advancing the argument with a judiciously selected quote; AO2 for the close analysis of the language and for discussing how form shapes meaning*].

- This sense of illogic might have been mitigated if Shylock acknowledged here – as Antonio does in the play's opening scene – that the ships are in different locations, thereby spreading the risk; yet this line of reasoning is conspicuously absent.[1]

- *Elsewhere in the play*: Significantly, this is not the only occasion in which the internal logic of a Shylock speech fails to add up. In Shylock's 'If you prick us' speech, Shylock seems to be making a logical, humanitarian argument in favour of treating all men equally. However, as his speech reaches its denouement, it abruptly and disorientatingly jumps to attempting to justify revenge.

Theme/Paragraph Three: However, while this speech may seem to lack internal logic, there is arguably a broader rationale underpinning it: namely, that Shylock is secretly plotting a revenge that depends on Antonio defaulting on his loan.

- Just after this extract, Shylock reveals his deep enmity towards Antonio: he asserts in a quiet aside that 'I hate him for he is a Christian.' Indeed, as the play unfolds, it becomes clear in retrospect that the bargain brokered in this scene – that Antonio must sacrifice a pound of flesh should he default on his loan – was in fact a premeditated act of revenge. With this in mind, the seeming internal illogic of the speech suddenly gains a strange, topsy-turvy logic: Shylock's gambit is, after all, entirely dependent on Antonio being *in*sufficient, on him 'squander[ing]' his wealth 'abroad,' and thus defaulting on his loan. [*AO1 for advancing the argument with a judiciously selected quote; AO2 for the close analysis of the language*].

- That a Jewish character might have been portrayed as deploying his powers of rationality for ill would have seemed apt to Shakespeare's audience, since they had been exposed to a number of anti-Semitic depictions that portrayed just that – for instance, the scheming villain of Christopher Marlowe's play, *The Jew of Malta*. [*AO3 for invoking relevant literary and historical context*].

- *Elsewhere in the play*: However, while the motive for revenge provides a rationale for many of Shylock's actions, his hunger for revenge is so extreme that it may be considered irrational in and of itself. In Act 4 Scene 1, as Antonio faces the prospect of Shylock's knife, Antonio's depiction of Shylock's stubbornness takes on transcendental proportions: he argues that trying to reason with Shylock is like 'stand[ing] upon the beach / And bid[ding] the main flood bate his usual height.' [*AO1 for advancing the argument with a judiciously selected quote*].

Theme / Paragraph Four: Shylock here is talking in prose; however, immediately after this extract, as Antonio enters, Shylock adopts a more formal

iambic pentameter. This shows his rationality as a social operator, since he is tailoring his patter for the interlocutor in question.[2]

- Prose appears in Shakespeare's plays generally in more informal circumstances, and usually in the mouths of those from a lower social strata, whereas iambic pentameter is frequently deployed in more serious circumstances, more often in the mouths of the higher born. However, in the same way Hamlet adopts prose when conversing informally with the high-born Rosencrantz and Guildenstern, Shylock, understanding the informal nature of this pre-negotiation with Bassanio, adopts a prose style that rationally reflects the conversation – Shakespeare using form to provide insight into Shylock's character. Shylock enhances this sense of informality with his diction: his 'Oh, no, no, no, no' a snapshot of everyday vernacular. [*AO1 for advancing the argument with a judiciously selected quote; AO2 for discussing how form shapes meaning*].
- *Elsewhere in the play*: However, when Antonio enters and more serious negotiations get underway, Shylock adopts a more formal iambic pentameter. Again, Shylock, behaving rationally in line with social mores, adopts the appropriate speech patter for the circumstance.

Conclusion

Again, we have a meaty essay here, so I'm not interested in introducing further themes in the conclusion. Instead, I shall seek to pick up any remaining AO3 marks going spare with a last titbit of historical context, then will use this as a spring-board for tying together the essay's thematic discussion:

"In 1594, Queen Elizabeth's Jewish doctor, Roderigo Lopez, was implicated in a plot to kill the queen. Although one must be careful not to overstate the public awareness of Lopez's Jewishness, it surely fed into an anti-Semitic stereotype of Jews as paradoxically both logical and illogical: logical in their methods, wildly illogical in their treasonous ends. In Act 4 Scene 1, Shylock concedes that he can 'give no reason' for plotting against Antonio, other than 'a lodge hate and a certain loathing.' Shylock is brutally logical in his scheming; however, whether his 'reason' for plotting against Antonio can be considered rational and proportionate is far less certain."

An illustration from H. C. Selous depicting
Bassanio and Antonio entreating Shylock
for a loan.

READ THE FOLLOWING EXTRACT FROM
ACT 2 SCENE 2 OF THE MERCHANT OF
VENICE AND ANSWER THE QUESTION
THAT FOLLOWS.

At this point in the play, the blind Gobbo is attempting to find Shylock's home in order to visit his son, Launcelot. However, unbeknown to Gobbo, he has bumped into his son nearby Shylock's home.

LAUNCELOT

But I pray you, ergo, old man, ergo, I beseech you, talk
    you of young Master Launcelot?

GOBBO

Of Launcelot, an't please your mastership.

LAUNCELOT

Ergo, Master Launcelot. Talk not of Master Launcelot,
    father; for the young gentleman, according to Fates
    and Destinies and such odd sayings, the Sisters
    Three and such branches of learning, is indeed
    deceased, or, as you would say in plain terms, gone
    to heaven.

GOBBO

Marry, God forbid! the boy was the very staff of my age,
my very prop.

LAUNCELOT

Do I look like a cudgel or a hovel-post, a staff or a prop?
Do you know me, father?

GOBBO

Alack the day, I know you not, young gentleman: but, I
pray you, tell me, is my boy, God rest his soul, alive
or dead?

**Starting with this passage, explain how
Shakespeare uses comedy in *The Merchant
of Venice*.**

Write about:

**• how Shakespeare uses comedy in this
extract**

**• how Shakespeare uses comedy in the play
as a whole**

Introduction

"Whereas Greek dramatists sought to keep distance
between comedy and tragedy, Shakespeare
experimentally yoked these genres, placing Hamlet in
the company of clowning gravediggers and threatening
the comic hijinks of *Much Ado About Nothing* with
the brooding Don John. The interplay between
comedy and tragedy is at the heart of *The Merchant of*

Venice, too: comic yet vaguely cruel deceptions – such as Launcelot feigning his death – offer insight into the play's more tragic deceptions, while also offering relief from the intensity of these tragic proceedings."

Theme/Paragraph One: Comedy in the play – particularly when deception is a key ingredient – is presented as a weapon that characters use to attack and goad one another; however, as this extract demonstrates, this weapon is prone to backfiring.

- At the crux of this extract is a cruel joke: Launcelot seeks to deceive his 'sand blind' father into believing that he is talking to a stranger, and that his son is in fact dead – 'or, as you would say / in plain terms, gone to heaven.' Sure enough, the deception induces distress in the 'old man:' he invokes God – 'God forbid' – and conveys that his son was a vital source of succour in his old age: 'the boy was the very staff of my age.' The way Launcelot histrionically takes umbrage at being referred to as a 'staff' – and insensitively (albeit comically) seems to insinuate that his distressed father had been making a phallic joke – demonstrates a callous disregard for his father's feelings.[1] [*AO1 for advancing the argument with a judiciously selected quote; AO2 for the close analysis of the language*].
- *Elsewhere in the play*: This sequence finds echoes in Portia and Nerissa's deception of Bassanio and Gratiano involving the rings in the play's final scene.

Again, the deception, while comic, is deployed as a tool to goad and attack, as the women call into question the men's fidelity.

- However, unlike Portia and Nerissa's gambit, Launcelot's gag backfires: although he attempts to disillusion his father – 'Do you know me father?' – Gobbo fails to understand ('is my boy...alive or dead?') and, to Launcelot's escalating frustration, remains confused well beyond this extract. The way this gag backfires powerfully prefigures Shylock's far more tragic experience in the play – Shylock's gambit against Antonio, after all, ultimately backfires. It also hints at a karmic force at work in the play that ensures ill will begets ill tidings. [*AO1 for advancing the argument with a judiciously selected quote*].

Theme/Paragraph Two: Shakespeare deploys comedy as a release valve that defuses the intensity of the plot's more tragic elements.

- The play's structure nestles this comic interlude between a slew of high intensity sequences: Shylock's sinister bargain and Morocco's failed courtship appear just beforehand, and Jessica and Launcelot's heartfelt farewells in the scene immediately afterwards. As such, this sequence functions to provide comic relief: an opportunity for the audience to catch their breath. The way comedy slows the play's proceedings can also be seen on a granular level. As Launcelot gears up to deliver his deception, he inserts a meandering interpolated clause that invokes 'Fates and Destinies' and other such esoterica, thus forcing both Gobbo and the audience to wait for his trick to get underway.

Moreover, by employing prose, Launcelot does away with the line-breaks that characterise iambic pentameter, further creating a sense of interminability. [*AO1 for advancing the argument with a judiciously selected quote; AO2 for discussing how structure and form shapes meaning*].

- Not only is comedy used to slow the plot, but in fact the prevarication becomes a source of humour in its own right. This form of humour is deployed again shortly after this extract when Launcelot seeks employment from Bassanio: Launcelot, hindered by his father, absurdly takes some twenty lines to cut to the chase.

- *Elsewhere in the play*: Whereas this sequence, despite its hint of cruelty, is a decisively comic interlude, there are other occasions when comedy intrudes on serious proceedings in a way that in fact escalates tensions. When Bassanio articulates his distress at Antonio's predicament in Act 4 Scene 1, and suggests he would sacrifice his wife to save him, the disguised Portia's quippy reply – 'your wife would give you little thanks' – only amplifies the sense of impending doom. [*AO1 for advancing the argument with a judiciously selected quote*].

Theme/Paragraph Three: Comedy is used as a way to highlight intelligence: Launcelot's wordplay and comic inventiveness in this extract marks him out as an agile thinker.

- The linguistic prowess Launcelot demonstrates as he sets up his prank hints at another use of comedy: as a means of highlighting intelligence. Particularly illuminating is Launcelot's play on the word 'father'. Given that he initially conceals the fact he is Gobbo's son, the audience recognises that when he first deploys the moniker 'father,' he uses it *not* literally, but as a seeming mark of respect for the older man: 'Talk not of Master Launcelot, father.' However, both Launcelot and the audience of course understand that Gobbo *is* his father, and that Launcelot is being anything but respectful; as a result, by using the word in this context, Launcelot packs a comic punch while also demonstrating his erudite grasp on irony. [*AO1 for advancing the argument with a judiciously selected quote; AO2 for the close analysis of the language*].

- While it is has already been noted that Launcelot reeling off esoterica generates comedy, it also demonstrates Launcelot's intellect: he conjures up diffuse allusions with impressive rapidity, invoking not only 'Fates and Destinies,' but also other symbols of destiny, 'the Sisters Three and such branches of learning.' Lorenzo later observes Launcelot's fondness of a 'tricksy word:' 'tricksy' not only suggests a penchant for deception and comic play, but also implies a level of skill. That comedy requires skill was widely appreciated in Elizabethan England, where expert comics, known as "roarers," would engage in insult competitions. [*AO2 for the close analysis of the language; AO3 for invoking relevant historical context*].

- <u>Elsewhere in the play</u>: If Launcelot's mastery of comedy highlights his intelligence, the same holds true for Portia. When, in Act 1 Scene 2, she comically observes how one of her suitors 'bought his doublet in

Italy his round hose in France... and his behaviour everywhere,' her hyperbolic depiction not only exhibits a sharp eye for detail, but also a genius of eloquence, since her turn of phrase is infinitely more memorable than a mere acknowledgement of the suitor's erraticism.[2] [*AO1 for advancing the argument with a judiciously selected quote*].

Conclusion

In this instance, I have one final theme I'd like to sneak into the conclusion: namely, that comedy in the play is also used as a tool to point out the play's fictionality. However, instead of simply spelling this out, I'm going to invoke another Shakespeare play, as this will allow me to pick up a few AO3 (context) marks while I'm at it.

"In *King Lear*, the spurned Edgar, concealing his identity, pretends to lead his blind father atop a cliff to facilitate his suicide.[3] While this scene's tragic gravity might set it apart from our comic extract, both draw attention to their plays' fictionality: they force the audience to acknowledge that, whereas these fathers are unable to see, the audience and the plays are defined by their capacity to see and be seen respectively. Yet if comedy in *The Merchant of Venice* also has a metafictional function – and its litany of women dressed as men in a winking nod to the men who played women on the Elizabethan stage confirms that it does – its function is more profound still.[4] Comedy, after all, is not a mere facet of the play; it is a 'very prop' that underpins it."

Shakespeare's home in Stratford-upon-Avon

READ THE FOLLOWING EXTRACT FROM
ACT 2 SCENE 6 FROM THE MERCHANT OF
VENICE AND ANSWER THE QUESTION
THAT FOLLOWS.

At this point in the play, the disguised Jessica is fleeing Shylock's home in order to elope with Lorenzo.

JESSICA
Here, catch this casket; it is worth the pains.
I am glad 'tis night, you do not look on me,
For I am much ashamed of my exchange:
But love is blind and lovers cannot see
The pretty follies that themselves commit;
For if they could, Cupid himself would blush
To see me thus transformed to a boy.
LORENZO
Descend, for you must be my torchbearer.
JESSICA
What, must I hold a candle to my shames?
They in themselves, good-sooth, are too too light.
Why, 'tis an office of discovery, love;
And I should be obscured.

LORENZO

So are you, sweet,
Even in the lovely garnish of a boy.

> **Starting with this extract, discuss how Shakespeare presents romance in The Merchant of Venice.**
>
> **Write about:**
>
> • **how Shakespeare presents romance in this extract**
>
> • **how Shakespeare presents romance in the play as a whole**

Introduction

Again, I shall kick things off with some historical context in a bid to score AO3 marks, though this time I plan to augment it by invoking a separate poet who inspired Shakespeare. I shall then, once again, give a rundown of the themes I intend to cover:

> 'While Italian poets, particularly Petrarch, had an outsized impact on how Elizabethans viewed and understood romantic love, Venice was first and foremost in the contemporary English imagination a place *not* of romance, but of male-centric commerce.[1] As a result, it is perhaps unsurprising that in the Venice of Shakespeare's play, as seen in this passage, romance

becomes a deeply transactional phenomenon, and possesses distinct homoerotic undercurrents..'

Theme/Paragraph One: Romantic relationships in the play are presented as overshadowed by financial concerns: courtship – in particular, the securing of a wife – is presented as a key means by which a Venetian gentleman might come by wealth.

- At this passage's outset, Jessica is quick to invoke the casket containing the wealth plundered from her father: 'Here, catch the casket.' Not only does this give the casket's presence structural emphasis, but the symbolism of Lorenzo grasping the casket before he has Jessica at his side is a hint that the treasure was the primary aim of his courtship. When Jessica observes 'it is worth the pains,' she is most obviously alluding to the physical strain of catching the casket. However, there is a sly second meaning at play: one that Jessica likely does not intend, yet the audience hears all the same – namely that, because of the wealth she brings with her, it is worth the pains for Lorenzo to couple up with an ethnic outsider. The word 'worth' is particularly loaded, since it threatens to assign a monetary value to the 'pains' Lorenzo endures. [*AO 1 for advancing the argument with a judiciously selected quote; AO2 for the close analysis of the language and for discussing how structure shapes meaning*].
- Again, the transactional nature of the relationship is reiterated when Jessica expresses how she is 'much

ashamed of [her] exchange.' On the most literal level, she is referring to the way she has exchanged her usual garb for that of a male torchbearer. However, there are again other resonances to the word 'exchange' – chief among them, the sense that her journey from Shylock's home to Lorenzo's bed is as much a financial arrangement as a romantic one. [*AO2 for the close analysis of the language*].

- *Elsewhere in the play*: The idea that the romance in male-female relationships is ancillary to male economic expediency is a recurring motif.[2] Bassanio makes clear his courtship of Portia is predicated on a desire to clear his debts – 'my chief care / is to come fairly off from [my] great debts' – and, in an uncanny parallel, the clearing of those debts is heralded by the securing of a casket. [*AO1 for advancing the argument with a judiciously selected quote*].

Theme/Paragraph Two: Romance within Venice often appears to be deeply steeped in homoeroticism. Lorenzo and Jessica are one of Venice's few heterosexual couples – but even then, Jessica's male garb can be construed as a nod to the prevailing homoerotism that pervades the city.

- In this sequence, Shakespeare takes pains to draw attention to Jessica's male garb. For one thing, Shakespeare has Jessica explicitly bemoan her disguise: she asserts that 'Cupid himself would blush / To see me thus transformed to a boy' – indeed, the line 'to see me thus transformed to a boy' invites the actor to assign three syllables to the word 'transformed' to have the line adhere to the iambic pentameter, placing aural emphasis on the line.[3] For another, the stagecraft – which places 'a candle' in Jessica's hand – renders Jessica's garb a visual focal point. Finally, Lorenzo himself speaks of Jessica's 'lovely garnish of a boy' – the phrase 'lovely garnish' subtly hinting that the garb itself possesses some eroticism for Lorenzo. [*AO1 for advancing the argument with a judiciously selected quote; AO2 for the close analysis of the language and for discussing how form shapes meaning*].

- Moreover, Jessica's line here is arguably a metafictional joke on Shakespeare's part – in Elizabethan England, female parts were played by men on the stage, and Shakespeare often alluded to this fact (such as when, in *Antony and Cleopatra*, Cleopatra fears that a young male actor might someday 'boy [her] greatness'). By inserting this metafictional reference, Shakespeare again puts emphasis on the maleness of this sequence. [*AO3 for invoking historical & literary context that offers relevant insight*].

- *Elsewhere in the play*: Shakespeare's Venice is an overwhelming male domain, and in many respects, the relationship between two Venetian men – Antonio and Bassanio – is the play's most convincing romantic relationship: Antonio is portrayed as lovesick from the start, and Bassanio openly admits that '[his] wife, and all the world / Are not with [him] esteemed above [Antonio's] life.' With this in mind, the cross-dressing in this passage no longer seems incidental. Shakespeare appears to be indicating that this heterosexual pair implicitly understand the city's homoeroticism, and are disguised as homosexual lovers in tacit acknowledgment. [*AO1 for advancing the argument with a judiciously selected quote*].

Theme/Paragraph Three: Insofar as this scene is presented as a courageous and daring undertaking, it might be argued that Shakespeare is presenting romance as inextricably bound up with epic and heroic acts.

- At the start of Act 5, Lorenzo and Jessica invoke a range of classical love stories involving night-time derring-do – ranging from Troilus climbing the 'Troyan walls,' to Thisbe braving a lion – before linking these to their own romance: 'In such a night / Did Jessica steal from the wealthy Jew.' In doing so, Lorenzo and Jessica offer commentary on the events of the extract, implicitly suggesting it represents a heroic and daring undertaking on par with the classical canon. It invites us to read the night-time circumstance of the elopement ('glad 'tis night') as a symbol of daring, and to see yet another meaning – namely, courage – in the assertion that the undertaking is 'worth the pains.' [*AO1 for advancing the argument with a judiciously selected quote; AO2 for the close analysis of the language*].
- Yet while the lovers in Act 5 seek to frame their romance in a certain light, the events in this extract seem in danger of becoming an unhappy parody of those daring romances of classical lore. Lorenzo turns up late, and, in this moment of betraying her father, Jessica's overwhelming emotional state is one of

shame: she describes herself as 'much ashamed;' talks of holding 'a candle to my shames' – the plural suggesting it goes beyond just cross-dressing; and describes her shames as 'too too light.' [*AO1 for advancing the argument with judiciously selected quotes*].

- One is reminded of how Bassanio frames his voyage to woo Portia as akin to Jason's courageous mission to capture the golden fleece in Greek myth – a portrayal that is emphatically undercut when Portia later reveals the prosaic nature of the journey with talk of the 'common ferry / Which trades to Venice.'[4] Thus romances in the play, particularly heterosexual one, are often characterised as daring and epic by the lovers themselves, yet Shakespeare ultimately seems to present them as parodies of such courageous romances. [*AO1 for advancing the argument with a judiciously selected quote*].

Conclusion

Yet again, I want to invoke a second play in order to score AO3 marks – yet, on this occasion, I'm planning to do so in a way that allows me to make a point about form, and thus pick up any remaining AO2 marks going spare.

This extract is greatly reminiscent of a sequence involving another of Shakespeare's Italian couples: Juliet visually appears above Romeo in the first act of *Romeo and Juliet* – just as Jessica does above Lorenzo here – and there is a back and forth between the lovers, mirroring the dialogue's form in this passage. Yet whereas Romeo and Juliet exchange heartfelt emotions, and Romeo is taking a genuine risk, any loving sentiments in this extract are overshadowed by the casket full of treasure and the cross-dressing, and any sense of danger undercut by Jessica's shame. Romance in Venice is thus greatly 'transformed' from the romance of Verona.[5]

An entrance into the historic Jewish ghetto in Venice.

READ THE FOLLOWING EXTRACT FROM
ACT 3 SCENE 1 OF THE MERCHANT OF
VENICE AND ANSWER THE QUESTION
THAT FOLLOWS.

At this point in the play, Tubal – another Jewish Venetian man – is informing Shylock of Jessica's departure, and of Antonio defaulting on his loan.

TUBAL

There came divers of Antonio's creditors in my
company to Venice, that swear he cannot choose
but break.

SHYLOCK

I am very glad of it: I'll plague him; I'll torture him: I am
glad of it.

TUBAL

One of them showed me a ring that he had of your
daughter for a monkey.

SHYLOCK

Out upon her! Thou torturest me, Tubal: it was my
turquoise; I had it of Leah when I was a bachelor: I

would not have given it for a wilderness of
monkeys.

TUBAL

But Antonio is certainly undone.

SHYLOCK

Nay, that's true, that's very true. Go, Tubal, fee me
an officer; bespeak him a fortnight before. I will
have the heart of him, if he forfeit; for, were he
out of Venice, I can make what merchandise I
will. Go, go, Tubal, and meet me at our
synagogue; go, good Tubal; at our synagogue,
Tubal.

**Starting with this extract, discuss how
Shakespeare presents friendship in *The
Merchant of Venice*.**

Write about:

• **how Shakespeare presents friendship in
this extract**

• **how Shakespeare presents friendship in
the play as a whole**

Introduction

'Considering that in sixteenth century Venice the
Jewish population was ghettoised by government
mandate – indeed, the word *ghetto* originates from the
forced sequester of Jews in Venice – it is perhaps

unsurprising that Shylock has Jewish acquaintances. Although Shylock and Tubal are considered outsiders by the play's Christian contingent, their friendship reflects many of the play's other friendships: Tubal gives Shylock a forum to lay bare his emotions and discuss the opposite sex, while the seeming inequality in their friendship echoes the play's other asymmetric friendships.'

Theme/Paragraph One: Shakespeare presents friendship as a forum in which individuals might lay bare their most extreme and candid emotions, and disclose difficult truths.

- Perhaps the most striking aspect of this exchange is the bluntness with which the truth is spoken and the rawness of Shylock's emotional response. Tubal delivers both the good and bad news (at least as far as Shylock is concerned) with an equal lack of ceremony: Tubal reports that 'the divers of Antonio's creditors' have told him that Antonio 'cannot choose but break' his bond, but also that they have shown him the ring they 'had of [Shylock's] daughter for a monkey.' That both of these nuggets of news are delivered in short, single sentences enhances the sense that Tubal, regardless of the content of his missive, delivers information with equal directness and candour. [*AO1 for advancing the argument with a judiciously selected quote; AO2 for discussing how form shapes meaning*].

- *Elsewhere in the play*: Shakespeare's presentation of friendship as a forum for truth-telling is evident in other friendships in the play, too: for instance, in the

dynamic between Bassanio and Gratiano, and the way
Bassanio at one point tells Gratiano that he is 'too
wild, too rude and bold of voice.' [*AO1 for advancing
the argument with a judiciously selected quote*].

- Yet if Tubal's truth-telling is a mark of the honesty
that characterises his friendship with Shylock, so too
is Shylock's willingness to lay bare his most intimate
emotions. The way Shylock tempestuously repeats
how 'glad' he is at Antonio's defaulting, and
brandishes his excitement to exact revenge ('I'll
plague him; I'll torture him'), points to an astonishing
emotional openness, while the word 'plague,' given its
echoes of the biblical plagues Moses unleashed on
Egypt while liberating the Jews, is a word uniquely
loaded in a conversation between two Jewish men.[1]
Moreover, the use of form – namely, the prose
employed throughout the exchange – emphasises the
candour and lack of affectation that characterises the
friendship. [*AO1 for advancing the argument with a
judiciously selected quote; AO2 for the close analysis
of the language*].

**Theme/Paragraph Two: Shakespeare presents
friendship as a domain in which power dynamics
and hierarchies are borne out: it appears in this
extract that Tubal is doing Shylock's bidding.**

- Although the frankness with which Tubal delivers his
missives can be construed as a sign of his honest
companionship, the very fact he is serving as a conduit
for such information suggests a power exchange:
Tubal appears to be acting as though Shylock's
messenger. This sense that Tubal is in Shylock's

charge is reinforced by the litany of instructions Shylock issues at the end of this extract: 'Go, Tubal, fee me an officer;' 'Go, Tubal;' 'go, good Tubal.' That these instructions come, structurally, just before the end of the scene allows the stagecraft to lend them further gravitas: Tubal leaves the stage at Shylock's command. [*AO1 for advancing the argument with a judiciously selected quote; AO2 for discussing how structure shapes meaning*].

- *Elsewhere in the play*: Shakespeare's presentation of friendship as a domain in which power-exchanges play out can be seen also between Portia and Nerissa, Portia's waiting-woman. Nerissa is in Portia's charge and Portia explicitly issues her directions: for instance, she commands Nerissa accompany her on her cross-dressing jaunt to Venice. Yet, like Cleopatra's women-in-waiting in *Antony and Cleopatra*, Nerissa also serves at Portia's confidante and bosom-buddy.

- However, while Shylock appears to be commanding Tubal in this extract, it ought to be noted that their relationship in the play is far less clear than the one that exists between, say, Portia and Nerissa. Tubal, after all, has lent a portion of the money that Shylock has lent to Antonio, implying that in fact Shylock is in the deferent position. At one point, Jessica refers to Tubal and another Jewish man as Shylock's 'countrymen,' suggesting a parity of power.

Theme/Paragraph Three: Shakespeare implies there is a fine line and deep similarity between friendship and enmity. Both friendship and hatred are characterised by powerful emotions, and

Shakespeare presents the transition from one to the other as surprisingly easy.

- In this extract, as Tubal divulges his news, Shylock expresses both intensely positive and negative feelings towards Tubal: he exhibits elation – 'I'm glad of it' – and resentment: 'Thou torturest me Tubal.' Shylock of course understands that Tubal is merely the messenger, and thus the flash of hatred arguably implied in the accusation of torture ought not to be overstated. However, the quick oscillation between love and hatred hints at a key dimension of friendship in the play: that it is a surprisingly close cousin to hatred. This is best illustrated when, in Act 1 Scene 2, Antonio and Shylock broker their deal, and Antonio spurns the idea that he might be Shylock's friend – 'lend it not / As to thy friends' – and opts instead to be Shylock's enemy: 'lend it rather to thine enemy.' Implicit here is how easily one might slip into either friendship or enmity: only a fine line separates these two states of similarly high-flown emotions.

- Interestingly, Shylock in this extract claims he 'will have the heart of [Antonio].' Of course, Shylock is talking with grotesque literality. However, one might imagine Bassanio talking of metaphorically having 'the heart of' Antonio. The symmetry between the language of hate and love seems to confirm their proximity: indeed, Shylock and Antonio almost seem to love to hate one another, their enmity arguably more effective in binding them than friendship.

Theme/Paragraph Four: Shakespeare presents the

friendship between men as oftentimes revolving around the discussion of women.

- Although the heart of Shylock and Tubal's conversation appears to be Antonio – or, more specifically, Antonio's heart – there is another key focal point in the dialogue: the women in Shylock's life. They are brought to mind as a result of the ring Tubal spotted in one of the creditor's possession, since, as Shylock explains, 'I had it of Leah when [he] was a bachelor' – that is, it was a gift from his now-deceased wife. Yet the object also implicitly invokes Shylock's prodigal daughter, Jessica, as she was the one who traded away the ring. Crucially, however, by invoking these women, Shylock and Tubal exemplify a key trait of male friendships throughout the play: that they very often revolve around the discussion of women.

- *Elsewhere in the play*: The pattern holds firm throughout the play: Lorenzo talks to his male friends about Jessica; Launcelot Gobbo and Lorenzo discuss the nameless 'Moor' Launcelot has impregnated; and Gratiano discusses Nerissa. Indeed, even Bassanio and Antonio's homoeroticism-tinged friendship is sustained by talk of Portia.

Conclusion

Although I already have four themes, I feel compelled to sneak in one last one – that Shakespeare in the play often presents friendships as being forged along ethnic lines. However, I shall use this as a springboard to make a final reference to historical context, and thus pick up any AO3 marks going spare.

'Given that Shylock twice here mentions 'our synagogue,' one might surmise that yet another facet of friendship in the play is that it is forged along ethnic lines: Jews fraternise with Jews, Christians with Christians. Yet this pattern is problematised by Jessica's friendship with Launcelot: Jessica, it seems, is acceptable as a convert – a notion that would have been familiar in Elizabethan London, where Jews who had renounced their religion were accepted. Yet while Jessica and Launcelot's friendship in some ways represents an anomaly, the honesty in their dialogue and the asymmetry in their societal standings largely serves to confirm our observations on friendship.'

Venice's Rialto bridge. It was completed in
its current stone form in 1591.

ESSAY PLAN SIX

READ THE FOLLOWING EXTRACT FROM
ACT 4 SCENE 1 FROM THE MERCHANT OF
VENICE AND ANSWER THE QUESTION
THAT FOLLOWS.

At this point in the play, a court is deciding on whether or not to award Shylock a pound of Antonio's flesh.

PORTIA
A pound of that same merchant's flesh is thine:
The court awards it, and the law doth give it.
SHYLOCK
Most rightful judge!
PORTIA
And you must cut this flesh from off his breast:
The law allows it, and the court awards it.
SHYLOCK
Most learned judge! A sentence! Come, prepare!
PORTIA
Tarry a little; there is something else.
This bond doth give thee here no jot of blood;
The words expressly are 'a pound of flesh:'
Take then thy bond, take thou thy pound of flesh;

But, in the cutting it, if thou dost shed
One drop of Christian blood, thy lands and goods
Are, by the laws of Venice, confiscate
Unto the state of Venice.
GRATIANO
O upright judge! Mark, Jew: O learned judge!
SHYLOCK
Is that the law?

Starting with this extract, discuss how Shakespeare presents justice in *The Merchant of Venice*.

Write about:

• **how Shakespeare presents justice in this extract**

• **how Shakespeare presents justice in the play as a whole**

Introduction

'Throughout Shakespeare's corpus there is a persistent fascination with the fallibility of man-made institutions for administering justice: at one point in *King Lear*, for instance, the half-mad king observes that there is no difference between a judge and a thief: 'change places and, handy dandy, which is the justice, which is the thief?'[1] *The Merchant of Venice* possesses much of this scepticism, presenting courts as geared in favour of a Christian majority, and at the mercy of those who can best manipulate language. In addition, it also explores the drama that underpins the administering of justice, and how the court is cast as a kind of pseudo-stage.'

Theme/Paragraph One: Shakespeare presents human systems of doling justice as geared against racial outsiders, and in favour of Venice's majority Christian contingent.

- At the key turning point in this extract – as Portia disguised as the lawyer Balthazar introduces the caveat that Shylock must not 'shed / one drop of Christian blood' while extracting a pound of Antonio's flesh – what is perhaps most striking is the kind of blood that is protected: 'Christian blood.' Implicit here is the notion that Christians enjoy preferential treatment under the law – that, say, Jewish blood would not enjoy such protection. In light of Shylock's earlier plea for humane treatment – 'If you prick us, do we not bleed?' – the honing in on blood is particularly potent: tacit is a sense that, even though Jews may bleed, the Christian-biased law remains indifferent to this fact. [*AO1 for advancing the argument with a judiciously selected quote; AO2 for the close analysis of the language*].

- That the law, and thus the course of justice, is geared against racial and ethnic outsiders is further illustrated by the emphasis placed on Shylock's status as a Jew in this sequence. Gratiano's exclamation, 'Mark, Jew' – a remark given emphasis as an inverted spondaic foot – reminds the audience that Shylock's Jewishness is pivotally important in the legal arena.[2] [*AO1 for advancing the argument with a judiciously selected quote; AO2 for the close analysis of the language*].

- *Elsewhere in the play*: A more subtle sign of the justice system's antagonism towards outsiders is the way Portia is allowed to act as mediator. Of course, the court does not realise this is Portia. Nevertheless, her antagonism towards racial outsiders, as illustrated by her scathing assessment of Morocco earlier in the play ('the complexion of a devil'), combined with the fact she undergoes scarcely any vetting, remains a damning indictment. Indeed, such antagonism towards Jews was ingrained in Venetian society, as illustrated by the fact that Jewish people, from 1516 onwards, were forced to live in a ghetto that was locked and gated every evening. [*AO1 for advancing the argument with a judiciously selected quote; AO3 for invoking relevant historical context*].

Theme/Paragraph Two: Shakespeare, by revealing how the law can be manipulated through semantic play, presents the Venetian justice system as fallible. He calls into question whether human laws can ever truly provide justice, or will simply reward those who can best manipulate language.

- At two separate points in this extract, parties from either side of the legal tussle find themselves praising Portia-cum-Balthazar's legal interpretations.[3] First,

Shylock proclaims Portia a 'most learned judge'; then, a short speech later, Gratiano sings Portia's praises in almost the identical terms: 'O learned judge.' The reason for this abrupt reversal is that Portia, in the interim, has radically reinterpreted the chief phrase governing the bond between Shylock and Antonio: namely, that Shylock, in the event of Antonio defaulting, should be entitled to 'a pound of [Antonio's] flesh.' Initially she appears to interpret this as permitting Antonio's murder: 'cut this flesh from off his breast: / The law allows it.' Yet in the speech that separates Shylock and Gratiano's words of praises, she abruptly rules that the absence of any language concerning blood in this contract must tacitly mean that the spilling of any blood would invalidate the contract – and, 'by the laws of Venice,' ensure the confiscation of all Shylock's 'lands and goods.' [AO1 for advancing the argument with a judiciously selected quote; AO2 for the close analysis of the language].

- What is painfully clear here is that those who truly broker power in the legal system are *not* those people who write 'the laws of Venice,' but those who have the power to interpret them – in this instance, Portia. Shakespeare thus presents justice as vulnerable to subversion by those who can most persuasively spin the language of the law.

- Elsewhere in the play: There is irony – and an implied lack of justice – in the fact that, while Portia subversively reinterprets the language of commitment in Shylock and Antonio's bond, she is later intent (albeit ultimately in jest) in holding Bassanio to the letter of his commitment to never give up his wedding ring in the play's final act.

Theme/Paragraph Three: Shakespeare presents the court of justice as venue for drama and play-acting. As a result, Shakespeare presents the course of justice as a kind of drama, and the court as an metaphor for the stage.

- In the action that takes place just prior to this extract, Portia-cum-Balthazar goes out of her way to give everyone in attendance the false impression that she will be coming down on Shylock's side. Indeed, at the start of this passage, she continues in this vein, strongly insinuating to Shylock that the court will be ruling in his favour: she says 'the court awards' him Antonio flesh twice in quick succession. Although one might argue that Portia is prevaricating to give Shylock opportunity to take mercy, it seems undeniable that she is also doing so for dramatic effect. By structuring her approach in a way that first lulls Shylock into a false sense of security and convinces the Christian contingent of their defeat, she ensures that, when she finally unveils her loophole, it packs a more potent dramatic punch. [*AO1 for advancing the argument with a judiciously selected quote; AO2 for discussing how structure shapes meaning*].
- That Portia is putting in a dramatic performance is confirmed not only by her instruction to Shylock to 'Tarry a little, there is something else' – a line which sees Portia self-consciously inject drama by slowing the pace and building suspense – but also through the stagecraft: she is disguised as a man, thus quite literally performing in costume. Given that female

characters were played by male actors on the Elizabethan stage, Portia's cross-dressing (albeit in the opposite direction) would have further emphasised the sense that she is putting on a performance. [*AO1 for advancing the argument with a judiciously selected quote; AO2 for the close analysis of the language; AO3 for invoking relevant historical context*].

- The upshot of all the self-conscious drama underpinning Portia's role in this sequence is that it presents the justice system not necessarily as a mechanism for delivering justice, but as a venue for entertainment, a kind of analogue for the theatre – and justice itself as ancillary to drama, as merely a pretence for drama.

Conclusion

On this occasion, I'm hoping to smuggle one last thought into the conclusion. In short, because this essay focused so heavily on mankind's institutions for administering justice, I wanted to implant a quick comment on the nature of divine justice – or lack thereof – in the play:

'In *King Lear*, the utter lack of justice brought about by human means is exacerbated by the seeming indifference of the universe: as Gloucester observes, 'As flies to wanton boys, are we to the gods. / They kill us for their sport.' However, in *The Merchant of Venice*, one might surmise that if there is some divinity at play, it is in fact working in favour of the Christian contingent: after all, in a seeming act of god, Antonio's ships miraculously reappear in the final scene. Yet, crucially, the idea of justice ultimately proves a Gordian knot, for if Shylock had been allowed to take revenge, it would hardly have seemed just, either.[4] Nevertheless, Shylock's question at the extract's close – 'is this the law?' – seems almost a universal howl of incredulity at the inadequacy of the law to come close to providing justice.'

Another illustration from H. C. Selous - this time, depicting Portia disguised as Balthazar in the Venetian court.

At this point in the play, Portia and Nerissa are chastising Bassanio and Gratiano for giving away their wedding rings.

PORTIA
Let not that doctor e'er come near my house:
Since he hath got the jewel that I loved,
And that which you did swear to keep for me,
I will become as liberal as you;
I'll not deny him any thing I have,
No, not my body nor my husband's bed:
Know him I shall, I am well sure of it:
Lie not a night from home; watch me like Argus:
If you do not, if I be left alone,
Now, by mine honour, which is yet mine own,
I'll have that doctor for my bedfellow.
NERISSA
And I his clerk; therefore be well advised
How you do leave me to mine own protection.

GRATIANO

Well, do you so; let not me take him, then;

For if I do, I'll mar the young clerk's pen.

Starting with this extract, discuss how far Shakespeare presents Portia as a destructive individual.

Write about:

• **how far Shakespeare presents Portia as destructive in this extract**

• **how far Shakespeare presents Portia as destructive in the play as a whole**

Introduction

'Given that Elizabethan England was a deeply patriarchal domain, Queen Elizabeth's status as head of state represented a paradox: a woman with the power to create and destroy, yet hemmed in by male-centric societal codes. Portia – empowered by her astronomical wealth, her social standing and fierce intellect, yet shackled by her father's posthumous wishes – in some respects mirrors Elizabeth's nuanced position.[1] In this extract, as Portia plays a practical joke on Bassanio, she threatens to destroy her relationship, while also playing the part of fiction-creator extraordinaire.'

Theme/Paragraph One: In this extract, Portia is presented as destructive insofar as she seems to be sabotaging the relationship with Bassanio by threatening to sleep with the (fictional) doctor. In the name of humour, she is potentially doing real damage.

- Although Portia is playing a practical joke in this extract – she is threatening to sleep with the doctor to whom Bassanio gave away his wedding ring, yet who is of course none other than Portia in disguise – the directness of Portia's threat to 'have that doctor for [her] bedfellow,' and the emotionally charged spectre of cuckoldry it conjures, nevertheless threatens to do real damage to Portia's relationship with Bassanio.[2] Portia's assertion that she will 'not deny [the doctor] any thing' is potentially even more incendiary, since 'any thing' implies that Bassanio would not only be displaced sexually, but also financially and emotionally. That the joke has a very real destructive effect on Bassanio's emotional wellbeing in the relationship is hinted at by Gratiano's violent reaction in the extract – he is, after all, the subject of a parallel prank by Nerissa – but also in Bassanio's distress in the dialogue beyond this extract. [*AO1 for advancing the argument with judiciously selected quotes; AO2 for the close analysis of the language*].

- In the Elizabethan era, as a result of patriarchal pressures on men to maintain sexual dominion over their spouse, the threat of cuckoldry would have been considered all the more emasculating, and cuckolds – depicted as they were with horns paradoxically symbolising their inadequate virility – were widely mocked in the art of the era. [*AO3 for invoking relevant historical context*].

- <u>*Elsewhere in the play*</u>: It might be observed that Portia's behaviour in this extract appears all the more destructive when one recalls that, while playing the part of a lawyer in Act 4, she entrapped Bassanio into giving away the ring in the first place, mocking his pleas that he 'should neither sell nor give nor lose it.' Even though Portia's prank is revealed to be just that shortly after this extract, one wonders whether the entrapment and threat of cuckoldry has not done lasting damage.

Theme/Paragraph Two: However, while Portia's behaviour here might be considered destructive to her relationship, it can alternatively be regarded as highly creative. Portia, by dreaming up a practical joke involving fictional characters and a manufactured scenario, takes on the role not of destroyer, but of artist extraordinaire.

- Portia's first line in this extract – 'Let not that doctor e'er come near my house' – is steeped in comic irony: the audience understands that the doctor is nearer than Bassanio could imagine, as Portia and the doctor are one and the same person. Above all, this line draws the audience's attention to Portia's inventiveness: the fact she has dreamt up this fictional doctor, *and* his fictional 'clerk' (played by Nerissa); that, by cajoling the men out of their rings, she manufactured the entire prank. Indeed, the sheer quantity of dialogue assigned to Portia in this sequence – and throughout this prank as it unfolds beyond this extract – further emphasises, through the use of form, Portia's role as engine of creative invention. [*AO1 for advancing the argument with a judiciously selected quote; AO2 for the close analysis of the language and for discussing how form shapes meaning*].

- *Elsewhere in the play*: Portia's creative fiction-making has parallels with Launcelot Gobbo, who, in Act 2 Scene 2, plays the part of a fictional stranger when confronted by his blind father, and who creates a fictional scenario in which Launcelot has 'gone to heaven.' However, whereas Launcelot's fiction-making suckers his father in just temporarily, Portia's creativity and fiction-making impressively spans multiple acts, winning the credulity of almost the entire play's *dramatis personae*.

Theme/Paragraph Three: Shakespeare presents Portia as at her most destructive when interacting with patriarchal power structures: throughout the play she challenges, and at times even bulldozes, the patriarchal power structures that order society.

- *Elsewhere in the play*: When Portia first appears in Act 1 Scene 2, though she is seemingly abiding by her father's demand that she marry the suitor who picks the right casket, there are already signs she is pushing back on the patriarchal demands that seek to bind her: she openly criticises not only the suitors, but also her father's stipulations ('a living daughter curbed by the will of a dead man'). Structurally, this early subversiveness prepares the audience for more of the same, and, sure enough, it could be argued that, when Bassanio later comes to choose a casket in Act 3 Scene 2, Portia undermines the casket stipulation by singing a song laced with clues pointing Bassanio towards the lead. [*AO1 for advancing the argument with a judiciously selected quote; AO2 for discussing how structure shapes meaning*].

- If the earlier portions of the play show Portia subverting her father's patriarchal power, this extract arguably sees her deconstructing the patriarchal power Bassanio supposedly wields as her husband. While her assertion that 'will become as liberal as you' is most obviously a threat to be as inconstant as Bassanio has been, in a broader sense it also suggests a gender reversal: Portia is threatening to usurp the liberality that is traditionally the domain of men. Indeed, by cross-dressing and entering the exclusively-male domain of Venetian law in the previous act, Portia has already done exactly what this line implies: usurped the domain of men.

- Moreover, her aforementioned threat to cuckold Bassanio, and her mocking remark that, in order to stop her cheating, he must 'watch [her] like Argus' – the hundred-eyed entity from Greek myth – constitutes a challenge to the patriarchal idea that a wife ought to be considered her husband's property: she is framing herself instead as a woman who is in all senses beyond the male regulatory gaze and thus its control. [*AO1 for advancing the argument with a judiciously selected quote; AO2 for the close analysis of the language*].

Conclusion

'In *Antony and Cleopatra*, the sardonic Enobarbus observes of Cleopatra that 'what she undid did' – a phrase that captures Cleopatra's paradoxical ability to destroy and create at once. This descriptor captures something of Portia, too: a woman who brazenly threatens to damage her relationship, and deconstruct patriarchal structures – so much so that she makes Gratiano's threat of phallic destruction levelled at his love-rival, 'I'll mar the young clerk's pen,' seem tame by comparison – while also functioning as the creator-in-chief, whose fictions reel in all and sundry.'

Street art rendering of Shakespeare in London

ENDNOTES

ESSAY PLAN ONE

1. An allusion is when a writer references something – for instance, a different work of literature or a work of art. In this context, the word 'classical' refers to art or literature that came from Greek or Roman civilisation. So a *classical allusion* is a reference to art or literature from Greek or Roman civilisation.

2. I imagine you are probably thinking: what is an unstressed hyperbeat? And perhaps even: what is iambic pentameter?

   Allow me to explain.

   Shakespeare's plays are almost entirely written in *iambic pentameter*. An iamb is a metrical foot in which the emphasis is on the second syllable, and tends to sound more like natural speech. A pentameter is when there are five metrical feet in a line.

   It is often easiest to illustrate with an example. If we take the second line of Bassanio's speech here, and use bold font to represent the stressed syllables, plus a vertical bar to indicate the end of each metrical foot, it will look like this: 'And **she** | is **fair** | and **fair**| er **than** | that **word**.' Since there are five metrical feet here, all iambic, it is rendered in iambic pentameter.

   An unstressed hyperbeat, however, is when there is an extra, unstressed syllable going spare at the end of the line.

   If we take the line we were discussing in the essay plan, and mark out the metre, it would look as follows: 'Her **name** | is **Por** | tia **no** | thing **un** | der **val** | ued.' As you can see, there are five consecutive iambs, then one extra, unstressed syllable going spare. This is the unstressed hyperbeat – though it used to be referred to as a "feminine ending."

   As an aside, when you have a stressed extra syllable, it is called a stressed hyperbeat (and, formerly, a "masculine ending").

3. The rack in fact predates the Elizabethan era. A torture victim would be shackled by their wrists and ankles, and their body then stretched by the rack.

ESSAY PLAN TWO

1. To mitigate is to make something less bad, or to alleviate something or a situation.

2. The interlocutor is the individual to whom a narrator or a person is talking.

ESSAY PLAN THREE

1. To be histrionic is to be over-the-top dramatic, or indeed melodramatic. A phallus is a penis, or a representation of a penis. To make a phallic joke, then, is to make a penis joke. In other words, Gobbo is likening his son, and the support he offered him, to a walking stick, and Launcelot is pretending that he believed Gobbo was referring to him as a penis.
2. Hyperbole is another word for exaggeration.
3. At the start of *King Lear*, Edgar's father, Gloucester, is tricked by his other son – the illegitimate Edmund – into believing that Edgar was conspiring against him, thereby forcing Edgar into exile. As a result of his lack of faith in Edgar and Edmund's continued duplicity, Gloucester winds up violently blinded and ejected from his home.
4. If a work of art is metafictional, it means that it is intentionally drawing the audience's attention to its own fictionality and artifice.

ESSAY PLAN FOUR

1. Petrarch was an Italian poet who lived in the fourteenth century, and whose fondness for sonnets had a huge impact on Shakespeare. The influence is perhaps most obvious in *Romeo and Juliet*, which contains a number of sonnets.
2. If something is ancillary to something else, it means that it is secondary.
3. On first reading, it appears the line contains just nine syllables, since 'transformed' would ordinarily be pronounced with two syllables.

   However, while Shakespeare, when writing in iambic pentameter, occasionally employs eleven syllable lines that finish with either a stressed or an unstressed hyperbeat, it is far more rare for him to fall short of the iambic pentameter altogether and use nine syllables. As a result, it is most likely that Shakespeare would have wanted the word 'transformed' to have been pronounced with three syllables, thereby bringing it in line with the iambic pentameter. Here's how it scans when we assign three syllables to 'transformed,' with bold font representing the stressed syllables, and a vertical line representing a break between each metrical foot: 'To **see** | me **thus** | trans**form** | ed **to** | a **boy**'
4. If something is prosaic, it means that it is everyday and unexceptional in nature.
5. Verona is the Italian city in which most of *Romeo and Juliet* is set.

ESSAY PLAN FIVE

1. The Book of Exodus – part of the old testament of the bible – tells of the Jewish people's enslavement in Egypt, and their liberation by Moses, who unleashes ten plagues on the Egyptians in order to secure his people's freedom.

ESSAY PLAN SIX

1. A writer's corpus is their collected works.
2. We have discussed how you get an iambic foot when you have a metrical foot comprising of two syllables, with a stress on the second syllable but not the first. A spondee, on the other hand, is when both syllables are stressed.

   Let's look at Gratiano's line here in more depth – and, as I've done elsewhere, mark out the stressed syllables with bold font and breaks between metrical feet with vertical lines: 'O **up** | right **judge**! |**Mark, Jew**: | O **learn** | ed **judge**!' As we can see, whereas all the other feet are iambs, the third foot here is a spondee. As a result, we might call it a spondaic foot. And because it differs from the predominant pattern, we can call it an 'inverted' foot.
3. 'Cum' in 'Portia-cum-Balthazar is a Latin phrase. It is usually used to describe two characteristics about a certain individual – for example, Barack Obama is a lawyer-cum-politician, and Portia is both Portia and, at least temporarily, the fictional lawyer Balthazar.
4. The Gordian knot appears in stories about Alexander the Great – it was a knot that supposedly could not be untangled. It is now proverbially used as a metaphor for an unsolvable problem.

ESSAY PLAN SEVEN

1. If something is posthumous, it means it takes effect after the person who designed it or put it in place has died.
2. A cuckold is a man whose wife has had sexual intercourse with another man.

AFTERWORD

To keep up to date with Accolade Press, visit https://accoladetuition.com/accolade-press. You can also join our private Facebook group (where our authors share resources and guidance) by visiting the following link: https://rcl.ink/DME.

Printed by Amazon Italia Logistica S.r.l.
Torrazza Piemonte (TO), Italy